THE MOLE FAMILY'S CHRISTMAS

The Mole Family's Christmas

by Russell Hoban

pictures by Lillian Hoban

SCHOLASTIC INC.

New York Toronto London Auckland Sydney

ISBN 0-590-45611-3

12 11 10 9 8 7 6 5 4 3 2 1   11   1 2 3 4 5 6/9

Printed in the U.S.A.   23

Harley Mole and his son Delver did straight mole work. They tunneled and they dug and they brought home the groceries. Harley and Delver wore overalls and thick boots and heavy work gloves. They wore thick glasses, because the whole Mole family was very nearsighted, and they had little lanterns in their caps, because they tunneled in the dark.

They tunneled in the springtime and the summer.

They tunneled through the fall and through the winter, while Harley's wife Emma cooked and cleaned and washed the overalls. All three of them worked every single day, and all days were the same for them.

In the evenings Emma mended overalls and
work gloves while Harley and Delver cleaned
the lanterns and scraped the mud from their
boots and rubbed them down with tallow.

When Delver's chores were done he polished up and sorted his collection of good-shaped stones and marbles and bits of colored glass that he had found while tunneling. And sometimes he just sat around and thought. "Delver is a brooder," Emma used to say to Harley.

"Delver is a thinker," Harley always answered. "There's no telling what that boy might do when he puts his mind to something."

The Mole family's home was under the lawn
of a house that had been empty for a long time.
But that fall a family of people moved in. And
that winter, very early one morning when
everyone was still asleep, Delver tunneled up
through the earth and snow to have a look
around.

At the back door of the house he found a house mouse looking at a calendar the milkman had left with Season's Greetings from the dairy. "Christmas is coming," said the mouse, and ran into his hole.

Delver thought about it all day, and at dinner he asked his mother and his father, "What is Christmas?"

"I have no idea," said Harley. "No idea whatever."

"Neither do I," said Emma. "Perhaps it's a people thing."

Delver thought about it some more, and that evening when his chores were done he went up to the people house. There he found the mouse again, dining on birdseed that had fallen from a feeder.

What is Christmas?" Delver asked him.

"Several different flavors of paper and cardboard," said the mouse. "Fresh paste sometimes, and no end of ribbon, string, and nesting materials. Constant footsteps overhead, and no rest for anyone until he's come and gone."

"Until who's come and gone?" said Delver.

"Fat man in a red suit," said the mouse. "White beard. First there's a lot of stomping and snorting and jingling up on the roof.

Then he comes puffing and wheezing down the chimney, puts knicknacks and candy in stockings, leaves all kinds of packages around, says 'Ho ho ho,' and goes huffing and puffing up the chimney again. It's quite an odd thing, really, but he does it only once a year, and nobody seems to mind."

"What's in the packages?" said Delver.

"Skates and trains, dolls and whatnot," said the mouse. "The people children write letters, and if they've been good the fat man brings them what they ask for."

Does he bring you anything?" asked Delver.

"No," said the mouse. "But then it's not my chimney, and I don't write letters. It's late," he said, "and I've got to be getting home before Ephraim Owl comes by on his evening rounds. Lovely night, isn't it? Look at all those stars!"

"Where?" said Delver.

"Up in the sky," said the mouse. "Where else?" He shook his head and ran back into the house.

Delver looked up, but he was too nearsighted to see the stars. When he squinted hard he could just barely make out a blurry brightness here and there, but that was all. He was still squinting up at the sky when a lady mouse came to nibble at the birdseed. "The stars are especially fine tonight, aren't they?" she said.

"They certainly are," said Delver.

"Indeed," said the lady mouse, "it's almost like singing, you might say, the way they glimmer and shine, isn't it?"

"Yes," said Delver, "I think it is," and he went on squinting while the lady mouse went on nibbling. After a while Delver said, "Do you have any particular way of looking at the stars?"

I just look up," said the lady mouse. "Of course I have seen people looking at them with telescopes, which is, I suppose, a particular way of looking. Look out!" she cried, and dove into the shrubbery, pulling Delver with her as old Ephraim Owl swooped down upon them.

Hoo hoo!" said Ephraim as he flew up with nothing in his talons. "If not this time, then some other time," and he flew away, hooting and chuckling.

"You'd better keep your eyes open," said the lady mouse to Delver. "He almost caught you."

I was thinking," said Delver. "What's a telescope?"

"I believe that a telescope is something like an extra, very far-sighted eye," said the lady mouse, "which would undoubtedly be helpful to anyone who might be somewhat nearsighted."

"Undoubtedly," said Delver. "Thank you very much. Goodnight." And he tunneled slowly home, thinking about the stars.

All the next day as Delver worked with his father he thought about the stars he could not see, and after a while he began to cry. "What's the matter?" said Harley, and Delver told him about the stars. "I went above ground a time or two when I was young," said Harley. "I heard about stars too, and I know how you feel."

"There are telescopes," said Delver, and he told his father what the lady mouse had told him. "I wish I had a telescope," said Delver.

So do I," said Harley. "It would be nice to see a few stars, just for the experience of it, you know."

"Maybe if we had a chimney," said Delver, and he told Harley about the fat man in the red suit.

"Ah," said Harley, "but that's a people thing. I never heard of a red-suited fat man giving anything to animals."

"And anyhow, we haven't got a chimney," said Delver.

W e've got a stovepipe," said Harley, "same as any other animals."

"You've got to have a chimney," said Delver.

"A people-sized chimney?" asked Harley.

"Well," said Delver, "it would have to be big enough for his hand with the telescope, at least."

"All right," said Harley, taking a deep breath and drawing himself up to his full height, "we'll make a chimney."

When Emma was told about the project she had many doubts. "I'd like to see the stars as much as anyone else," she said, "but we mustn't get our hopes too high." Nevertheless she threw herself wholeheartedly into the work.

The Mole family made many nighttime trips above ground for sand and cement for their mortar. Harley and Emma and Delver carried pieces of broken brick and heavy stones, always watching and listening for the owl. Old Ephraim failed to catch them night after night, but vowed that he would soon or late dine upon them. "The longer it takes," he said, "the better you'll taste." But the Moles kept working on their chimney in spite of Ephraim, and every night it grew higher.

The mouse who had told Delver about Christmas showed him how to spell out the words for his letter, and by the time the chimney was half built he was ready to mail it. The question was where to? "I know he comes down," said the mouse, "so he must come from *up*. If I were you I'd send the letter up."

So the Moles found a very long stick and stuck it straight up in the snow, with the letter in a cleft at the end of it. The letter said:

To the fat man in the red soot–
All of us Mols down here hav bin good.
We need a telaskop so we can look at the
stars. Maybe you dont giv things to aminals.
Well then I will swop my ston marbel and
glass colleckshun for it. If that is not enuf
my father and I could work out the diffrens
in tunels or plane digging if you need enny
tunels or plane digging dun.

                       Your friend,
                       Delver Mol

That night the Moles stopped work before
Old Ephraim made his rounds, and so they
were in bed when he passed overhead on silent
wings. Old Ephraim saw the letter on the stick,
snatched it up in his talons, stuck it in his back
pocket, and flew away with it.

When the Moles came out the next night and saw that the letter was gone they were all very pleased. "Well," said Delver, "now that it's been picked up, it's just a matter of time till the telescope comes."

Then the Moles worked very hard every night to finish their chimney. All of them hoped very much that the fat man in the red suit would come, but each of them thought that perhaps he might not come.

So just to make sure that Delver and Harley
would have something for Christmas, Emma
knitted new mufflers for them. Harley made a
pair of pretty slippers for Emma and a pair of
moccasins for Delver. Delver made a sewing box
for his mother and a reading lamp with a green
ginger-ale-bottle-glass shade for his father.

Then all the Moles wrapped their presents and hid them. "Even if the fat man doesn't bring the telescope," said Emma to Harley and Delver, "he may leave some other little presents, you know."

"Just what I was thinking," said Harley.

"So was I," said Delver, and all three of them smiled to themselves.

When the Moles finished the chimney by the light of the moon on Christmas Eve they were all exhausted. They sat on top of their chimney and sighed happily, smiling up at the stars they could not see, and they were so tired that they all fell asleep sitting there in a row.

They were still sitting there asleep when old Ephraim flew over. "Hoo hoo!" said Ephraim. "There they are like a three-course dinner, all ready and waiting for me. I'll just swoop down, and they'll jump up and run—but they won't be fast enough."

Ephraim swooped down, but the tired Moles stayed fast asleep. "This doesn't seem quite right," said Ephraim, and he flew up again. "I'll hoot very loudly and count to ten to give them a head start and then I'll catch them.

"Hooo!" he hooted. "Wake up!" But the Moles would not wake up.

Silly things!" said Ephraim. "They write letters about telescopes and stars and they sleep out in the open by the light of the moon. They certainly *deserve* to be eaten!"

Just then the midnight bells rang out in all the churches in the town, and the sound floated on the still air over the sparkling snow. Then from high up under the silent-singing stars there came a faint jingling of sleigh bells, and all at once old Ephraim felt very jolly and full of fun. "Wouldn't those Moles feel foolish if they woke up and found themselves not eaten!" he chuckled. "And maybe just for fun I'll give that letter to whoever it is way up there in a sleigh. Maybe *he* knows the fat man in the red suit."

So it was that on Christmas morning the Moles woke up feeling very foolish for having fallen asleep out in the open, and found themselves not eaten. And there beside them on the chimney was a beautiful, shining telescope.

"You see," said Delver, "all it took was a chimney, and I didn't even have to swap my stone, marble, and glass collection!"

But the joke wasn't only on the Moles, because when Old Ephraim woke up that afternoon he found a nicely wrapped package inside the door of the hollow tree where he lived. Inside the package was an elegant striped necktie, and a card that said:

Season's Greetings to a jolly good fellow from the fat man in the red suit.

Best regards,
S. Claus

So that was the Mole family's first Christmas, and they were very pleased with it. On top of the chimney they made an owlproof observatory out of an upside-down flower pot, and then they were able to look at the stars in perfect comfort. "I think Delver did very well to find out about Christmas as he did," said Emma.

Yes," said Harley, "you never can tell what will happen when a boy like Delver puts his mind to something. Here am I, who never expected to see a single star, looking at all of them. I call that impressive."

"It really *is* like singing, the way they glimmer and shine," said Delver.

Even Delver's mouse friends, who were not
at all nearsighted, found that they enjoyed
viewing the stars through a telescope, and now
they visit the Moles' observatory often.

Old Ephraim wears his necktie constantly,
and although he still hunts the Moles regularly
he has not yet managed to catch them.

There has been talk of using the Mole chimney next Christmas for all of the local animals, and the mice are already at work on their letters to the fat man in the red suit. So is Old Ephraim, who—being somewhat more knowledgeable—will address his letter to S. Claus.

The End